D1320729

Grandma Georgia's Amazing Handbag

By
K.D. Greaves

Grosvenor House
Publishing Limited

This book is published by
Grosvenor House Publishing Ltd
Link House
140 The Broadway, Tolworth, Surrey, KT6 7HT.
www.grosvenorhousepublishing.co.uk

A CIP record for this book
is available from the British Library

Paperback ISBN 978-1-80381-231-1
Hardback ISBN 978-1-80381-232-8

*How many times can you
find me in the story?*

Illustrated
by
Roberta Magro

When Grandma Georgia came to visit, she always brought her old, battered handbag with her.

What's happening to the clasp on Grandma Georgia's bag?

Klara was very curious about Grandma's handbag. It was midnight blue with sparkly stars and a large, silver clip in the shape of a crescent moon.

How many stars are on Grandma's bag?

From Grandma Georgia's bag came wonderful things… Sweets and colouring books for Saturday visits. Cards and presents on birthdays. Chocolate bunnies, fluffy chicks and painted eggs at Easter.

What would you choose from the bag?

Buckets, spades and bouncy beach balls
for holidays.

*Can you name the
colours on the beachball?*

11

Brightly wrapped gifts and shiny tree ornaments at Christmas Time.

How many baubles are on the tree?

Klara didn't know how one bag could
hold so many things.

*What can you see outside
the window?*

So she climbed inside to find out.
And fell…

*Do you think I'll follow
Klara into the bag?*

and fell…

Were you right?

and fell...

*What do you think
Klara's saying?*

As she fell, Klara tumbled past row after row of shelves. On the shelves were sweets, chocolates, toys, books, cards, clothes and decorations all neatly labelled. "Now I know how Grandma Georgia's bag holds so much," Klara said. "It's magic."

Which things inside the bag are yellow?

Then Klara had another thought –
how *deep* was the bag? "I wonder
how long before I reach the bottom?"
she said to herself. "Perhaps there isn't
one. Perhaps I shall keep on falling
forever?" Klara started feeling
frightened. She began to cry.

*Can you name all the
things in the picture?*

Just then, a hand on a long arm popped down from above. Klara found herself travelling up and up and up and…

Two things in the picture have a dotty pattern on them. Can you find and name them?

…OUT of the bag, onto Grandma Georgia's lap. Grandma Georgia mopped up Klara's tears with a big yellow handkerchief covered in red spotted ladybirds. She smiled at Klara. "It's good to be curious, Klara," she said. "But always be careful."

Where else can you see a ladybird in the picture?

Then she pulled a big, sticky lollypop
out of her bag and gave it to Klara.
Klara stopped crying and felt better.

*What might a cat like
instead of a lollypop?*

She was still curious about Grandma Georgia's bag. But she never climbed into it again.

What might Klara be thinking?

Further discussion point

*What would you like to find
inside Grandma Georgia's bag?*

Ingram Content Group UK Ltd.
Milton Keynes UK
UKHW051317090723
424678UK00008B/73